Dear Reader,

Introducing... Caramba! We're excited to present this book to you as a gift from us to read and enjoy.

Caramba is a story about a cat that lives in a world where cats can fly. Like other cats, Caramba has soft fur and a long tail. He eats fish and purrs. While other cats can leap off of cliffs and can soar over the ocean, Caramba just cannot seem to fly. One day, Caramba's cousins take him on a lesson to teach him how to fly, but he falls into the ocean and finally discovers his own very special gift.

TD is proud to make this book available to you as part of the TD Grade One Book Giveaway — one of several children's reading programs we support each year. This year, every Grade One student in Canada will receive a copy of *Caramba*. We hope you enjoy reading it and that this will be the start of a lifelong adventure into the world of books.

Have fun reading!

Ed Clark

Ed Clark
President and CEO
TD Bank Financial Group

To Chapinouche, Ronron, Paul Pigeon, Loupiot and Mirò

Special edition prepared for the TD Grade One Book Giveaway Program.
This edition is published by special arrangement with the Canadian Children's Book Centre and TD Bank Financial Group for free distribution to Grade One children across Canada in celebration of the 2010 TD Canadian Children's Literature Awards.

Groundwood Books / House of Anansi Press
110 Spadina Avenue, Suite 801, Toronto, Ontario M5V 2K4
www.groundwoodbooks.com

The Canadian Children's Book Centre
40 Orchard View Blvd., Suite 101
Toronto, Ontario M4R 1B9
www.bookcentre.ca

Design by Michael Solomon
The illustrations are in watercolor, pencil and pastel.
Printed and bound in Canada by Friesens Corporation

Also available in French: *Caramba*

ISBN (English) 978-0-929095-64-6
ISBN (French) 978-0-929095-66-0

Library and Archives Canada Cataloguing in Publication

Gay, Marie-Louise
Caramba / written and illustrated by Marie-Louise Gay.

This edition is published by special arrangement with the Canadian Children's Book Centre and TD Bank Financial Group for free distribution to grade one children across Canada in celebration of the 2010 TD Canadian Children's Literature Awards.
ISBN 978-0-929095-64-6

I. Canadian Children's Book Centre II. Title.

PS8563.A868C37 2010 jC813'.54 C2010-901961-X

CARAMBA

written and illustrated by

MARIE-LOUISE GAY

GROUNDWOOD BOOKS HOUSE OF ANANSI PRESS TORONTO BERKELEY

Caramba looked like any other cat. He had soft fur and a long, stripy tail. He ate fish. He purred. He went for long walks.
But Caramba was different from other cats. He couldn't fly.

It worried him a lot.

“Every cat in the world can fly,” he said to Portia, his best friend, “except me.”

“I’m different, too,” said Portia. “I’m pink and fat. I have a curly tail…”

“You’re a pig,” cried Caramba. “All pigs are pink and fat.”

“…and I can’t fly, either,” said Portia.

“Pigs don’t fly. Cats do,” sighed Caramba. “Everyone knows that.”

It was true.
Soon after they learned to walk, young cats would begin to fly.
They would leap off the cliffs and soar over the ocean.

Caramba watched them swoop and glide and skim the waves.
"That looks like fun," said Portia. "Don't you even want to try?"
"No," said Caramba.

But secretly Caramba did try.
He jumped off a small rock…
and fell flat on his face.
“What are you doing, Caramba?” asked Portia.
“I’m looking for caterpillars,” mumbled Caramba, his mouth full of grass.
“For my caterpillar collection.”

Then Caramba leaped off a chair…
and landed in his grandpa's lap.
"Ay, Caramba!" cried his grandfather. "What are you doing?"
"I'm admiring your slippers," muttered Caramba. "They're very nice."

Caramba decided to try on a windy day.
He ran as fast as he could and flapped his arms.
“What are you doing up there, Caramba?” asked Portia.

“Just hanging around,” said Caramba, “waiting for my socks to dry.”
Finally, Caramba gave up.
“That’s it!” he told Portia. “I’ll never fly!”

"*What?* You can't fly?" said Bijou.
Caramba looked up. His heart sank.
His cousins, Bijou and Bug, were hovering just above his head, purring loudly.
"That's ridiculous," said Bug. "Every cat knows how to fly."
"Caramba can do other things," said Portia. "He collects caterpillars, he tells stories, he cooks cheese omelets…"
"But he can't fly!" laughed Bug.
"Caramba, what is wrong with you?"

Caramba didn't answer.
What could he say? That he was afraid to fly? That flying made him dizzy? That he had tried over and over again and failed every time?

The cats flew away, giggling and weaving between the clouds.
"Let's do something else," said Portia. "Let's go for a ride in the rowboat."
"I don't want to do anything else," said Caramba. "I want to be alone."

Caramba walked slowly down to the pier.
“What *is* wrong with me?” he thought. “Why am I different?”
He wondered how it would feel to fly –
to float like a cloud, to be light as a feather, to be free as a bird,
to be like all the other cats.
It probably felt wonderful.

Then, with a furry whirring noise, Bijou landed on the pier.
"I have an idea, Caramba," said Bijou. "We'll give you a flying lesson."
"What if you drop me?" said Caramba. "What if…"

“Don’t be such a scaredy-cat,” said Bug. “Cats are meant to fly.”
Bijou and Bug each grabbed one of Caramba’s paws.

Up they went. The wind whistled through their fur.
Birds swooped beneath them.
Caramba opened his eyes. He was amazed. He could see forever.

He could see forests and rivers, red roofs on tiny houses,
the patchwork squares of fields.
It was stupendous. It was scary.

Now the ocean glistened, moving like a giant animal stretching out beneath them.
“Are you ready?” asked Bijou.
Caramba’s throat was dry. “No!” he whispered.

But they didn't hear him. They let him go.
"Fly, Caramba!" cried Bijou. "Flap your arms! Whirl your tail!"
But Caramba fell like a stone into the dark water.

Bubbles rose around him.
Seaweed tickled his paws.
Caramba opened his eyes. Schools of fish were staring at him.

Crabs scuttled over the white sand.
Sea urchins and starfish basked in the blue light.
Caramba's fur waved softly in the water. He was floating!

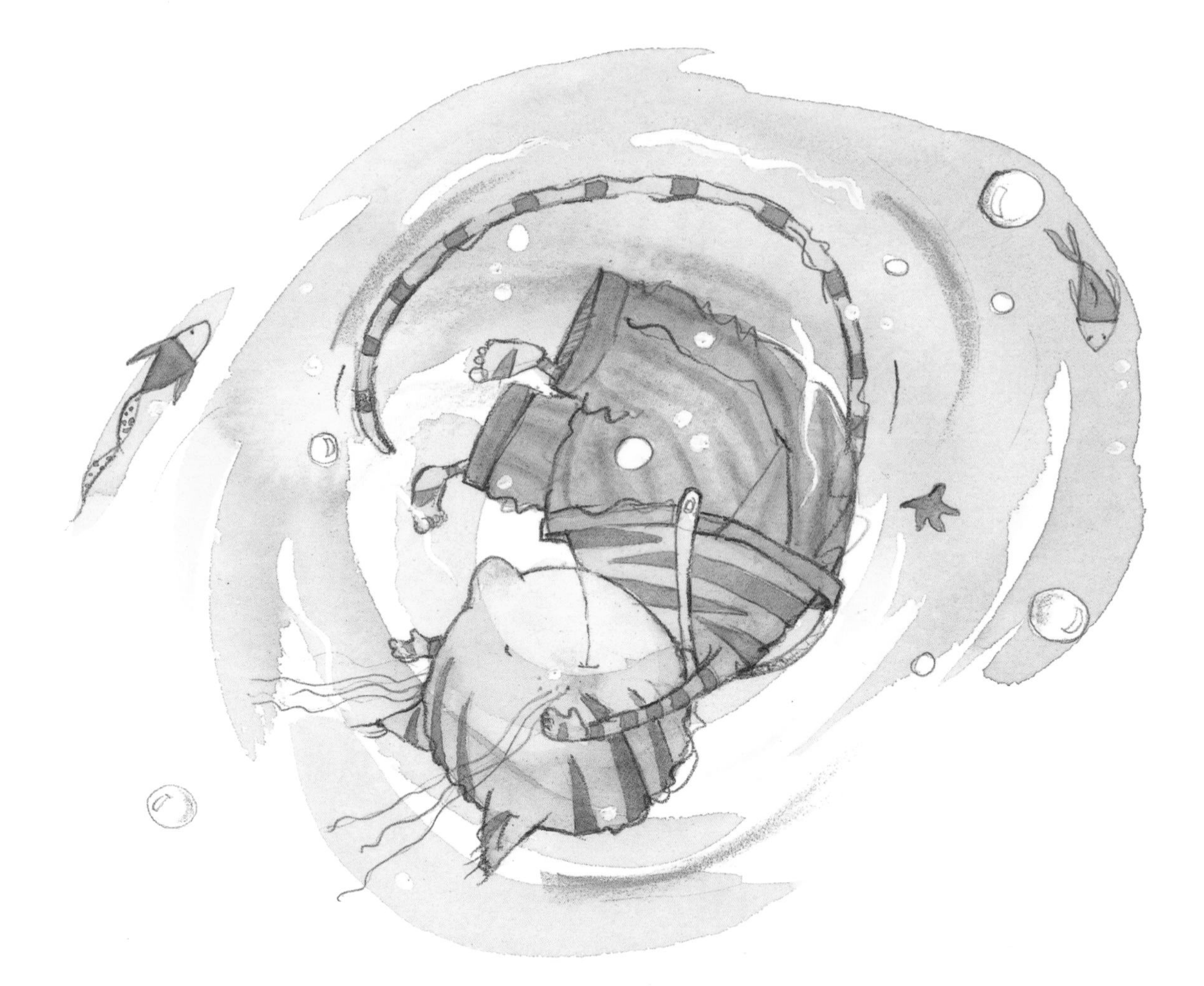

Caramba flapped his arms… and glided through the water.
Caramba whirled his tail… and soared through the seaweed.
He somersaulted and swooped.
He was light as a feather. Free as a bird.
It was like flying!

Up above, Portia, Bug and Bijou were very worried.
"Caramba!" they called. "Car-r-r-ramba!"
Suddenly Caramba popped out of the water. "I'm here!" he cried.

His cousins stared in amazement as he swam toward the rowboat.
“What are you doing?” cried Bijou “Cats can’t swim! Everyone knows that!”
“Well, I can,” said Caramba.

“How was it?” asked Portia.
“Wonderful!” said Caramba, drying his ears. “You should try it.”
“I just might,” said Portia. “Who knows? Maybe pigs can swim, too.”

Dear Reader: Here are some other great Canadian children's books.
The ones with a star (★) are suitable for readers ages 4 to 7.

2009 Award-winning Canadian Children's Books

ALBERTA BOOK ILLUSTRATION OF THE YEAR AWARD
Tara Langlois (illustration) and Dustin Delfs (photography). *Ollie's Field Journal: A 9/10ths Happy Story from Africa* by Patti McIntosh. Edmonton: Maggie & Pierrot, 2008.

ALBERTA CHILDREN'S BOOK OF THE YEAR AWARD
Patti McIntosh. *Ollie's Field Journal: A 9/10ths Happy Story from Africa.* Illustrated by Tara Langlois. Photography by Dustin Delfs. Edmonton: Maggie & Pierrot, 2008.

ALCUIN SOCIETY AWARDS FOR EXCELLENCE IN BOOK DESIGN IN CANADA
Robert Chaplin. *Brussels Sprouts & Unicorns: A Book of Rhymes.* Designers: Robert Chaplin and Sian Pairaudeau. Vancouver: Robert Chaplin, 2009.

AMELIA FRANCES HOWARD-GIBBON ILLUSTRATOR'S AWARD
★ Dušan Petričić. *Mattland* by Hazel Hutchins and Gail Herbert. Toronto: Annick Press, 2008.

ANN CONNOR BRIMER AWARD FOR CHILDREN'S LITERATURE
Jill MacLean. *The Nine Lives of Travis Keating.* Markham, ON: Fitzhenry & Whiteside, 2008.

ARTHUR ELLIS BEST JUVENILE CRIME AWARD
Sharon E. McKay. *War Brothers.* Toronto: Puffin Canada, 2008.

BLUE SPRUCE AWARD
★ Mélanie Watt. *Chester.* Toronto: Kids Can Press, 2007.

BOLEN BOOKS CHILDREN'S BOOK PRIZE
Penny Draper. *Graveyard of the Sea.* Regina: Coteau Books, 2008.

CANADIAN LIBRARY ASSOCIATION BOOK OF THE YEAR FOR CHILDREN AWARD
Anne Laurel Carter. *The Shepherd's Granddaughter.* Toronto: Groundwood Books, 2008.

CANADIAN LIBRARY ASSOCIATION YOUNG ADULT CANADIAN BOOK AWARD
Allan Stratton. *Chanda's Wars.* Toronto: HarperCollins, 2008.

CHOCOLATE LILY YOUNG READERS' CHOICE AWARD
★ (Picture Book) Chris Tougas. *Mechanimals.* Victoria: Orca Book Publishers, 2007.
(Chapter Book/Novel) Joan Betty Stuchner. *Honey Cake.* Illustrated by Cynthia Nugent. Vancouver: Tradewind Books, 2007.

CHRISTIE HARRIS ILLUSTRATED CHILDREN'S LITERATURE PRIZE
★ Katarina Jovanovic. *The King Has Goat Ears.* Illustrated by Philippe Béha. Vancouver: Tradewind Books, 2008.

DIAMOND WILLOW AWARD
Gordon Korman. *Swindle.* New York: Scholastic Press, 2008.

ELIZABETH MRAZIK-CLEAVER AWARD
Oleg Lipchenko. *Alice's Adventures in Wonderland* by Lewis Carroll. Toronto: Tundra Books, 2009.

FIRST NATION COMMUNITIES READ

★ Sylvia Olsen with Ron Martin. *Which Way Should I Go?* Illustrated by Kasia Charko. Winlaw, BC: Sono Nis Press, 2007.

GEOFFREY BILSON AWARD FOR HISTORICAL FICTION FOR YOUNG PEOPLE

John Ibbitson. *The Landing*. Toronto: Kids Can Press, 2008.

GOLDEN EAGLE CHILDREN'S CHOICE BOOK AWARD

David A. Poulsen. *The Prisoners and the Paintings*. Toronto: Key Porter Books, 2008.

GOLDEN OAK AWARD

Alma Fullerton. *Libertad*. Markham, ON: Fitzhenry & Whiteside, 2008.

GOVERNOR GENERAL'S LITERARY AWARDS

★ (Illustration) Jirina Marton. *Bella's Tree* by Janet Russell. Toronto: Groundwood Books, 2009.
(Text) Caroline Pignat. *Greener Grass: The Famine Years*. Calgary: Red Deer Press, 2008.

HACKMATACK CHILDREN'S CHOICE BOOK AWARD

(Fiction) Jennifer McGrath Kent. *Chocolate River Rescue*. Halifax: Nimbus Publishing, 2007.
(Non-Fiction) Ann Love and Jane Drake. *Sweet! The Delicious Story of Candy.* Illustrated by Claudia Dávila. Toronto: Tundra Books, 2007.

HALIFAX MAYOR'S AWARD FOR EXCELLENCE IN BOOK ILLUSTRATION

★ Eric Orchard. *The Terrible, Horrible, Smelly Pirate* by Carrie Muller and Jacqueline Halsey. Halifax: Nimbus Publishing, 2008.

INFORMATION BOOK AWARD

Janet Wilson. *One Peace: True Stories of Young Activists*. Victoria: Orca Book Publishers, 2008.

LILLIAN SHEPHERD MEMORIAL AWARD FOR EXCELLENCE IN ILLUSTRATION

★ Susan Tooke. *Up Home* by Shauntay Grant. Halifax: Nimbus Publishing, 2008.

MANITOBA YOUNG READERS' CHOICE AWARD

Christina Kilbourne. *Dear Jo: The story of losing Leah…and searching for hope*. Montreal: Lobster Press, 2007.

MARILYN BAILLIE PICTURE BOOK AWARD

★ Hazel Hutchins and Gail Herbert. *Mattland*. Illustrated by Dušan Petričić. Toronto: Annick Press, 2008.

McNALLY ROBINSON BOOK FOR YOUNG PEOPLE AWARD

★ (Children's) Joe McLellan and Matrine McLellan. *Goose Girl*. Illustrated by Rhian Brynjolson. Winnipeg: Pemmican Publications, 2007.
(Young Adult) Colleen Sydor. *My Mother Is a French Fry and Further Proof of My Fuzzed-Up Life*. Toronto: Kids Can Press, 2008.

MUNICIPAL CHAPTER OF TORONTO IODE JEAN THROOP BOOK AWARD

Linda Granfield. *Remembering John McCrae: Soldier • Doctor • Poet*. Toronto: Scholastic Canada, 2009.

NATIONAL CHAPTER OF CANADA IODE VIOLET DOWNEY BOOK AWARD

Budge Wilson. *Before Green Gables*. Toronto: Penguin Canada, 2008.

NORMA FLECK AWARD FOR CANADIAN CHILDREN'S NON-FICTION

Mariatu Kamara with Susan McClelland. *The Bite of the Mango*. Toronto: Annick Press, 2008.

QUEBEC WRITERS' FEDERATION PRIZE FOR CHILDREN'S AND YOUNG ADULT LITERATURE

Monique Polak. *What World is Left*. Victoria: Orca Book Publishers, 2008.

R. ROSS ANNETT AWARD FOR CHILDREN'S LITERATURE
★ Hazel Hutchins and Gail Herbert. *Mattland*. Illustrated by Dušan Petričić. Toronto: Annick Press, 2008.

RED CEDAR BOOK AWARD
(Fiction) L.M. Falcone. *The Devil, the Banshee and Me*. Toronto: Kids Can Press, 2006.
(Non-Fiction) Stanley Coren. *Why Do Dogs Have Wet Noses?* Toronto: Kids Can Press, 2006.

RED MAPLE AWARD
(Fiction) Norah McClintock. *Out of the Cold*. Toronto: Scholastic Canada, 2007.
(Non-Fiction) Elizabeth MacLeod. *Royal Murder: The Deadly Intrigue of Ten Sovereigns*. Toronto: Annick Press, 2008.

ROCKY MOUNTAIN BOOK AWARD
Eric Walters. *Safe As Houses*. Toronto: Doubleday Canada, 2007.

RUTH AND SYLVIA SCHWARTZ CHILDREN'S BOOK AWARD
★ (Picture Book) Mélanie Watt. *Chester's Back!* Toronto: Kids Can Press, 2008.
(YA-Middle Reader) Alma Fullerton. *Libertad*. Markham, ON: Fitzhenry & Whiteside, 2008.

SASKATCHEWAN BOOK AWARD
Karen Edwards. *One Cold Armpit*. Saskatoon: Art Department Saskatoon, 2009.

SCIENCE IN SOCIETY BOOK AWARD
(Youth Book under 16 Years) Carol McDougall. *A Salmon's Sky View*. Victoria: First Choice Books, 2009.

SHEILA A. EGOFF CHILDREN'S LITERATURE PRIZE
Polly Horvath. *My One Hundred Adventures*. Toronto: Groundwood Books, 2008.

SHINING WILLOW AWARD
★ Chris Tougas. *Mechanimals*. Victoria: Orca Book Publishers, 2007.

SILVER BIRCH AWARD
(Express) Alan Cumyn. *Dear Sylvia*. Toronto: Groundwood Books, 2008.
(Fiction) Mahtab Narsimhan. *The Third Eye*. Toronto: Dundurn Press, 2007.
(Non-Fiction) Kevin Sylvester. *Gold Medal for Weird*. Toronto: Kids Can Press, 2007.

SNOW WILLOW AWARD
Christina Kilbourne. *Dear Jo: The story of losing Leah... and searching for hope*. Montreal: Lobster Press, 2007.

STELLAR BOOK AWARD
Carrie Mac. *The Droughtlanders*. Toronto: Puffin Canada, 2006.

TD CANADIAN CHILDREN'S LITERATURE AWARD
★ Nicola I. Campbell. *Shin-chi's Canoe*. Illustrated by Kim LaFave. Toronto: Groundwood Books, 2008.

TIME TO READ: THE BRITISH COLUMBIA ACHIEVEMENT FOUNDATION AWARD FOR EARLY LITERACY
★ Mélanie Watt. *Chester*. Toronto: Kids Can Press, 2007.

WHITE PINE AWARD
Cory Doctorow. *Little Brother*. New York: Tor Books, 2008.

Photo by Gilbert Duclos

Marie-Louise Gay

Born in Quebec City, Marie-Louise Gay studied graphic design at l'Institut des arts graphiques in Montreal, animation at the Montreal Museum of Fine Arts School and illustration at the Academy of Art College in San Francisco. She has worked as an editorial illustrator, an art director and a production manager for a children's book publisher. Marie-Louise has written three puppet plays for which she created the sets, puppets and costumes. She has also designed clothes for children and created sets for an animated film at the National Film Board.

But for the past twenty-five years, Marie-Louise Gay has been writing and illustrating books for children. Although she didn't begin drawing until she was sixteen, she is now one of Canada's leading illustrators. She has taught illustration at the Université du Québec à Montréal, and she continues to give readings, workshops and talks in schools and libraries and at conferences across Canada, Europe, Mexico and the United States. She has won numerous awards for her work, including two Governor General's Awards, and she has been nominated for the Hans Christian Andersen Award and the Astrid Lindgren Memorial Award.

Marie-Louise Gay has written and/or illustrated over sixty books for children — board books, picture books and chapter books. *Stella, Star of the Sea*, the first book in her wildly popular Stella series, was published more than ten years ago. She has since written and illustrated four more Stella books and three books about Stella's little brother, Sam. They have been translated into fifteen languages, have received rave reviews and are loved by children all over the world. Her new book, *Roslyn Rutabaga and the Biggest Hole on Earth!* is an ode to the imagination and determination of children, who create their own worlds out of the little things in life.

Marie-Louise lives with her family in Montreal, Quebec.

The Canadian Children's Book Centre

Over 500,000 Grade One children across Canada will receive a copy of *Caramba* through the annual TD Grade One Book Giveaway Program, administered by the Canadian Children's Book Centre (CCBC) and funded by TD Bank Financial Group.

The Canadian Children's Book Centre is a national, not-for-profit organization that promotes the reading, writing and illustrating of Canadian children's books. The CCBC provides programs, resources, materials and activities that are used by teachers, librarians, authors, illustrators, publishers, booksellers and parents.

Best Books for Kids & Teens is the CCBC's annual selection guide to the best new Canadian books, magazines, audio and video. Each year, hundreds of recently published books and other resources are evaluated and selected by jury committees from across the country. *Best Books for Kids & Teens* highlights the best Canadian books to buy, borrow and read, making it a terrific resource for teachers, librarians, booksellers and parents to make informed selections for young readers.

Canadian Children's Book News, the CCBC's quarterly magazine, reviews books, interviews authors and illustrators, profiles publishers and bookstores, informs and updates readers about issues affecting children's education and reading, and provides information and news about the world of children's books in Canada.

The CCBC is also the organizer of TD Canadian Children's Book Week, the largest annual celebration of Canadian books and readings in schools and libraries across Canada. During Book Week, Canadian authors, illustrators and storytellers travel across the country, from coast to coast and up to the far north, visiting schools, libraries, community centres and bookstores to talk about their books and meet young readers. Book Week also inspires many independent activities and local celebrations of Canadian children's books and their creators.

For more information on the Canadian Children's Book Centre and the TD Grade One Book Giveaway Program, please visit our website at **www.bookcentre.ca**.

The Canadian Children's Book Centre
40 Orchard View Blvd., Suite 101
Toronto, Ontario M4R 1B9
Telephone: 416 975-0010
Fax: 416 975-8970
Email: info@bookcentre.ca

The Canadian Children's Book Centre
Bringing Canadian books and young readers together